# INSATIABLE

**By Evan Couchot**

NOVELS:
*Makan*
*Adverse Events (coming 2026)*

NOVELLAS:
*Insatiable*

# INSATIABLE

Evan Couchot

# Insatiable

Copyright © 2026 Evan Couchot

All rights reserved. No part of this book may be reproduced, distributed, or transmitted in any form or by any means, including photocopying, recording, or other electronic or mechanical methods, without the prior written permission of the publisher, except in the case of brief quotations embodied in critical reviews and certain other noncommercial uses permitted by copyright law.

This is a work of fiction. Names, characters, places, and incidents are a product of the author's imagination or are used fictitiously. Any resemblance to actual persons, living or dead, or actual events is purely coincidental.

**Published by Crypsis Press LLC**

Stoneham, Massachusetts

www.crypsispress.com

**First Edition: March 2026**

ISBN: 978-1-971827-01-8 (paperback)

ISBN: 978-1-971827-00-1 (ebook)

Library of Congress Control Number: 2026902370

# INSATIABLE

# CHAPTER 1

A FADED GREEN 2007 Honda Civic grumbled down the narrow dirt driveway underneath the depleting foliage of the overgrown trees on either side. The driveway wound like a brown snake through blowing grass, constantly changing course to avoid boulders and large tree trunks. The brown, yellow, and green leaves above were sparse, yet still managed to block most of the afternoon sun. There was a high-pitched scraping as the old car passed too close to a red maple with low, obtrusive branches.

"Can you even see where you're going?" Eric asked, not daring to take his eyes off the road as if him looking from the passenger seat was keeping them on course.

"Yes, for the most part," Marissa responded, hunched over the steering wheel with wide eyes.

"I can't see anything," Eric added.

"That's because you're colorblind and we're in the shade," Vanessa said from a slouched, careless position in the back seat. "It's not that dark out."

"No I'm not! It would just be easier to see if you got your headlights fixed," Eric mumbled.

"Are you paying for them?" Marissa questioned, briefly taking her eyes off the road to stare at Eric accusatorially.

He put his hands up in front of himself defensively. "What are the bedrooms like here?" he said, desperate for a distraction from the sketchy, never-ending road.

"Two bedrooms," Marissa began, keeping her eyes glued to the shaded driveway outside. "One has a queen and overlooks the lake. The other has a bunk bed and looks out into some trees."

"I wonder which one I get," Vanessa said while rolling her eyes.

"Do you want to switch?" Marissa replied, her voice tainted with annoyance.

"No, it's fine," Vanessa let out a deep sigh. "I'm the third wheel; I know my role."

The car continued its slow journey down the seemingly endless driveway until finally the trees opened up to a clearing. They squinted as the car pulled off the dirt and onto a paved section of driveway. There was a small yard on the right side, with a lone arborvitae growing about eight feet tall, next to a small shed of about the same height with red wooden accents on the doors. The paved driveway continued past the shed where it opened up into a wider portion for parking.

The cabin was straight ahead, two stories tall with gray siding and windows with the same red wooden accents as the shed. The cabin was simply shaped in the way a child would draw a house; a tall rectangle with a triangular roof, out of which a lone chimney peeked out puffing smoke. There were two front doors, one near the wall on each side. Beyond the cabin, the surrounding trees and landscape gave way in the sense that only an open body of water can explain.

The car paused for a few moments while the three within took in the view. It wasn't anything spectacular, but it was their home away from home for the weekend.

"Wait, is someone here?" Vanessa asked as they all noticed the white Jeep Wrangler Unlimited parked in an open section of pavement near the house.

"There shouldn't be," Marissa said as she pulled in next to the Jeep and parked. "Maybe the owner keeps a car here."

The three got out of the car just as someone came out of the left door. The man stopped, looked at the three confused, and then smiled.

"Yo Steve," he shouted. "Man, I told you this was a duplex!" The man looked to be in his mid-twenties and was wearing a Coors t-shirt and sweatpants. He had stubbles of a beard and medium-length brown hair that was messy on top but cleaner cut on the sides. He came out from the open door and walked towards the Honda. "Hey guys! You staying here this weekend?"

"Yeah," Marissa said, hesitantly.

"We thought it was just us," Vanessa stepped closer to the man, smiling up at him. "But I guess we're sharing."

The man smiled down at Vanessa when another, slightly shorter man came out of the left door. "What do you…" the new man's voice trailed off. "Ah, I see."

"So it looks like the cabin is split right down the middle," the first man spoke again. "I bet my friends a beer that we'd be sharing the place this weekend." His eyes drifted from person to person, and settled on Vanessa. "That's fine by me," he smiled again. "I'm Dylan." He stuck out his hand, first to Vanessa, who took it eagerly.

"Vanessa," she grinned back up at the tall man with broad shoulders.

"Eric." He moved in front of the two girls to shake Dylan's hand with a firm grip.

"Marissa." She gave an unenthusiastic wave just before Dylan could reach his hand in her direction.

"I'm Steve," the other man with carefully styled blonde hair and a beard waved from his position in between the door and the group. He was skinny, but some extra weight jiggled from his lower belly as he waved.

"Jesse's out in the woods somewhere looking for some good firewood for later."

"Well, we'll let you guys get settled," Dylan said. "If you guys need anything, let us know. Especially beer." He laughed at himself. "That's basically all we packed."

"And dice," Steve added as he turned around to head inside.

"And dice," Dylan confirmed, smiling again at Vanessa before turning around to follow Steve back into the cabin. Her eyes followed him the whole way.

"Really, Ness?" Marissa said when Dylan closed the door behind him.

"What?" Vanessa responded looking back at her sister.

"You know what you were doing," Marissa answered. "Can you just help us get everything inside before you start flirting with the neighbors?"

"Whatever," Vanessa said as Eric opened the trunk. He leaned in and grabbed a green hiking backpack stuffed with clothes and handed it to Marissa. Then he took out his own blue backpack and put it on. Vanessa leaned past him and grabbed her black and pink duffle bag.

"Need a hand with the cooler?" Marissa asked as Eric pulled the large white bin from the trunk.

"I got it," he answered before setting it down to close the trunk. He picked it back up, leaning backwards as he shuffled awkwardly towards the cabin door behind Marissa.

"I wasn't even doing anything," said Vanessa, unprompted.

Eric smiled. "You were giving him the big eyes."

"What does that even mean?"

"The big eyes," Eric began. "When a girl gets close to a guy and looks up with her eyes but not with her head." He demonstrated for their benefit.

"No I wasn't." Vanessa had a pouty look of denial on her face.

"I didn't know that was a term but yeah Ness, you were giving him the big eyes," Marissa confirmed.

"We can't all be in the perfect relationship," Vanessa said mockingly as Marissa unlocked the door and the three proceeded into the cabin. The door opened into a hallway. The first bedroom, with the bunk bed, was on the immediate right. Vanessa walked in apathetically.

Next was the bathroom, and across the hall from it was another door with a lock on it. The hallway went on for a little ways before opening into the dining room on the left, and the living room on the right. Straight ahead, the wall was mostly made up of windows revealing a gray-blue lake surrounded by woods, and a door that led to a small staircase down to the lawn and past that, the little dock floating on the water.

Parallel to the hallway on the left side was an enclosed flight of stairs that led to the master bedroom above. The kitchen was adjacent to the stairs and dining room, making it slightly around the left corner when coming from down the hall.

Eric set the cooler down gently on the floor of the kitchen. He and Marissa then went upstairs to see their room.

"ANYTHING GOOD OVER there, babe?" Marissa called from the kitchen as she unpacked the cooler and filled the fridge.

"Nothing I've ever even heard of," Eric responded as he perused the bookshelf in the living room.

"You brought your book though, right?"

"Of course, but you know I always like to look. I can't help it." Eric's long fingers ran across the spines of a couple paperbacks before stopping on a thick brown hardcover with scratchings of illegible text. He tilted it away from the rest with his index finger and looked at the tattered cover that was flaking away to reveal the yellowing pages underneath. It read *Algonquin Culture, Mythology, and Stories*. He flipped through the pages and walked to the living room. He sat down on the scratched, mud-colored leather couch which turned out to be surprisingly comfortable.

"Kichi Manido, Pagwadjinini, Widjigo," Eric read aloud.

"What are you saying?" Marissa crossed the dining room and sat down next to Eric with a whoosh of air leaving the old cushions.

"I have no idea," he answered and showed her the title of the book. "I guess they're Algonquin mythological figures or something. There's handwriting all over the pages too, like someone was taking notes."

"Creepy," Vanessa said from the hallway that led from the dining and living room area to the bedrooms and front door.

"What's creepy about it?" Eric asked.

"Oh not your Pagwa-widji-whatevers," Vanessa responded. "These pictures on the wall."

Marissa got up and looked at the pictures with her sister. "I see what you mean," She said with a smile. "There's a weird mix of black and white and regular color."

"Yeah and I can't figure out who is related to who," Vanessa added. Eric set the book down on the coffee table and got up to join the girls.

The three stood and stared at the many pictures on the wall. "I think this is the guy who owns the place," Marissa said, pointing at a man probably in his sixties that was standing with two Native American looking men. "At least it looks like Alan from his online profile when I booked the place."

Eric stopped staring to think for a minute. "Wait, Alan what?" he asked looking at Marissa.

"I forget," Marissa scrunched her face trying to remember. "I wanna say Robinson or something like that."

"Was it Alan Roberson?"

"Oh yeah, I think that was it," Marissa said confused. "How did you know?"

"There's like five books on the shelf by Alan Roberson," Eric answered. "Maybe this is like his author's getaway where he comes to write."

"Really?" Marissa walked to the bookshelf to see for herself. "Oh wow, you're right."

"You doubted me," Eric said smugly. Marissa smiled back at him and shook her head.

"Whoever he is, he's got a weird thing for Native stuff," Vanessa said. "My room has like a thousand dreamcatchers."

"Ours does too, now that you mention it," Marissa added.

"Woah this is a crazy looking one," Eric stared intently at a medium-sized black and white picture.

"What's crazy about it?" Marissa asked, coming back to check. "It looks like old Alan just sitting in a rocking chair with a very, very serious expression."

Vanessa was looking now too. "Oh, I see it now! It's one of the ones that the eyes follow you everywhere you move. Creepy." The three of them stood staring at the old man's eyes.

*KNOCK! KNOCK! KNOCK!*

They all jumped at the sudden, heavy sound that came down the hallway.

# CHAPTER 2

ERIC SLOWLY TURNED the doorknob and gently pulled. It stuck, forcing him to give a hard tug.

"Hey man!" Dylan was standing in the doorway holding a grilling spatula. "We're gonna hit the yard down by the dock and do some grilling and play some drinking games if you guys want to join."

Eric opened his mouth to respond but Vanessa's voice came from behind him. "That sounds so fun! We'll be down in a couple minutes!"

Dylan smiled and peered behind Eric for the source of the voice. He looked back to Eric, smiling with raised eyebrows.

"I guess we'll be down in a couple," Eric laughed and shook his head. "What are you guys grilling?"

"We've got some burgers and brats, Steve said he has a little asparagus apparently but I honestly don't know if he was joking."

"Mind if we toss some stuff on too?" Eric asked.

"Not at all, bring down whatever!" Dylan responded.

"Sounds good, I'll gather up the girls." Dylan nodded to Eric before he shut the door.

Shortly after, the girls were ready and the cooler was packed. Eric led them to the back door, while the girls grabbed the rest of the food behind him.

"Pretty nice place, don't ya think?" Marissa said as they looked out from the back windows and down to the yard and lake below.

"Not bad," Eric said, taking in the scenery. Two wooden stairways extended from small landings that came off of each side's back door. The back of the rustic cabin sat perched on stilts above the slight grassy slope that led to the flat yard below.

Where the yard met the lake there was a small, but sturdy looking wooden dock. Its weather-worn wooden planks were wide at the beginning but narrowed to about six feet wide where it extended a short distance onto the lake. There was a kayak tied up to the dock, bobbing up and down with the gentle waves. Every now and then there would be a deep *thunk* when it collided with one of the dock support beams.

Directly between the grassy yard and the little dock was the metal fire ring, already filled with wood and ready to be lit. Adirondack and camping chairs surrounded it, with a massive Yeti cooler between two of them.

To the right of the firepit was a large, property-spanning fence that was painted white in a previous life, but certainly not in this one. Stacked against it was a great pile of beautifully placed firewood, about the height of person and twice as long.

Left of the fire pit was a small gravel square, lined with old wooden beams. In the square there was a small wooden picnic table and a grill, currently being attended by Steve. The forest beyond it was an imposing dark wall where the sun barely penetrated a few yards past the grill, even in the bright daylight.

"Come on down!" Dylan called as he carried a plastic bag of red cups and a white folding table near the campfire and began setting up.

"We're coming!" Vanessa called back as she brushed by Eric and carried their food down towards the yard. Marissa slapped Eric on the butt and started down the stairs.

"Don't worry, I got it," Eric mumbled to himself as he turned sideways to hobble at an awkward angle down the stairs while carrying their cooler. He stumbled twice, but the cooler's bulk was enough to wedge him between the rails, preventing a fall. Eventually he made it to the ground and planted the cooler next to the grill. The girls were already lounging in chairs by the firepit.

"What is that?" Steve asked, face contorting as Eric placed two pale, frozen patties on the grill.

Eric shook his head and rolled his eyes before he called out, "Marissa, what did you say this was?"

"They're impossible chicken burgers!" she answered from her Adirondack chair near the inactive fire pit. She took a sip of her alcoholic tea drink. "They're really good and low calorie."

"Yikes, brother," Steve whispered to Eric. "Did you bring any real meat?"

"Doesn't seem that way," he answered bitterly.

"I'll tell you what," Steve kept his voice lower than necessary. "Jesse gets these beef patties from his special hometown butcher. Supposedly, they're American wagyu. I don't know if that's true but they're damn good. You're welcome to a couple of em."

"Really?" Eric's eyebrows raised. "That would be unreal, if you've got extras."

"We have plenty, don't even worry about it." Then he turned towards the others sitting around the firepit. "Hey Jesse, did you figure out the music yet?"

"I'm trying," The man with shoulder-length, midnight-colored hair stared down at his phone and a cylindrical portable speaker with frustration. "I'm definitely connected but…" His voice trailed off as he mumbled to himself. He wore jeans with legs cut off mid-shin and a tan and red flannel, unbuttoned to reveal a plain white shirt underneath.

"I don't think there's any service out here," Vanessa said, holding her own pink-cased phone above her head. "And the stupid cabin doesn't even have Wifi."

"Oh yeah, did the host send you that message too?" Steve asked from the grill.

"What message?" Eric stood holding a plate of still-frozen meat for Steve to add to the grill.

"Apparently the internet lines run all the way from the main road, like those 8 or 9 miles down the driveway," Steve gestured behind the house with his spatula hand. "And some animals burrowed down to them or dug them up or something and basically chewed them to shit last week. They haven't been able to send someone out to fix it yet."

"Great," Vanessa glared at her sister before sighing deeply and leaning back in her chair.

"Here," Dylan flicked his phone towards Jesse who expertly picked it out of the air and began switching the Bluetooth connection. It connected with a sudden deep whooshing sound. "I've got some playlists downloaded."

The music started as a quiet hum and gradually the volume and bass increased and increased until Jesse could feel the *thump, thumping* in his lap. He tapped his bare feet against the grass below.

"Ayyy!" Steve shouted, bending his knees and bouncing as he flipped some meat off the grill with extra flair.

"So how do you guys all know each other?" Marissa asked Jesse and Dylan by the unlit firepit. Vanessa was sitting in between Marissa and Dylan, but seemed to inch closer to Dylan each time she shuffled in her seat to get more comfortable.

"We went to college together," Jesse answered. He took a heavy drink, tipping his beer can completely vertical before leveling out and crushing it slightly between his fingers.

"And played soccer together," Dylan added.

"Oh, so you're athletic?" Vanessa asked, looking between the two guys. Marissa rolled her eyes.

"To some extent," Dylan laughed. "Though some say we were more of a drinking team with a hobby for soccer."

Vanessa and Marissa both laughed as Jesse cracked another beer and tapped it against Dylan's.

"Competitive might be the best word to describe us," Jesse said after finishing another heavy gulp. "But we'll show you that when we play games after dinner."

"What games do you have in mind?" Eric asked, carrying plates of food towards the conversation. He handed Marissa and Vanessa each double impossible chicken burgers with some floppy asparagus on the side. He grabbed a chair and moved it close to Marissa before sitting down with his own plate.

"Beer die is a favorite," Steve said as he joined the group, passing a plate with a burger and brat to Dylan.

"That's a good one," Eric said before stuffing food into his mouth.

"I think I put it together, but how do you all know each other?" Dylan pointed at each of them with his beer.

"We–" Marissa was interrupted.

"She's my sister," Vanessa said with a mouth full of food. She finished chewing, then swallowed. "And that's her lover, Eric."

Eric looked at Marissa with an incredulous smile and mouthed *lover?*

Marissa shook her head and rolled her eyes.

"They've been dating for a while so they're basically an old married couple," Vanessa added.

"And you?" Dylan asked.

"I'm perpetually single. Stuck third-wheeling until I die, it seems." Vanessa took another bite of her burger as she smiled at Dylan.

"Hey, that's okay. The three of us are single too," Jesse added in. "When our spirits meet the right counterpart, everything will work out."

"Spirits?" Marissa said, suppressing a chuckle.

Dylan laughed, taking another sip of his drink. "Jesse, here, thinks he's Native American. That's why you might see him wander off through the woods a few times this weekend."

"What do you mean 'thinks'" Jesse exclaimed. "You know I'm one sixteenth Native!"

"Jesse, where's the other pack of burgers?" Steve interrupted, looking towards them from the grill.

Jesse looked up from his beer in confusion. "Other pack?"

"You brought two, right?" Steve asked.

"No, just the one," Jesse said. "Are we out?"

Steve glanced over to Eric, who had already taken a few bites of his burger. Marissa looked at his plate for the first time. "What's that?"

"Uhh," Eric couldn't speak with his mouth full of food.

"Ohh," Jesse looked to Eric and back to Steve. "I guess we're out. What are you going to eat?" he asked Steve.

"Dude, I already ate like 5 brats and a burger. Perks of being grill master."

"So I'm the only one without food?" Jesse said, offense clear on his face.

"I think there's one more brat," Steve laughed.

"And more impossible chicken burgers," Eric added guiltily.

"Yeah, right. Thanks Dad and Grandpa," Jesse laughed, waving his hand first at Steve then at Eric. "You think these 170 pounds of built body can survive on one little brat?" He ignored the offer for impossible chicken burgers.

"Sorry I took your burger," Eric said.

"Don't worry about it," Jesse said with a smile. "It's good, right?

"It's honestly unbelievable," Eric answered mid-bite.

"They really are," Jesse said. "But no worries, party people. I'll just go take a peek inside and see what I can scrounge up." He got up from his seat with a quick lean and headed up the wooden stairs and into the right side of the cabin.

"If you don't see anything on your side, feel free to check ours while you're up there," Eric called after him.

"Thanks!" Jesse called back as he was running up the steps toward the back door.

"He's really 170 pounds?" Vanessa asked with a teasing voice and a smile.

Steve and Dylan laughed. "On a good day. He's pretty skinny for that tall frame." Dylan opened the cooler and tossed a beer to Steve.

Eric opened their own cooler between him and Marissa and grabbed a beer. "So, you guys play any other games?"

"Ever heard of chesties?" Dylan asked.

"No," Eric answered before taking a swig of his beer.

"It's kind of like beer pong but your partner is diagonal from you and you have to bounce the ball to them. They have to use their chest to hit the ball in the cup."

Marissa's face brightened and she hit Eric in the shoulder. "That's titty pong!"

"Oh, you've told me about that," Eric said, giving her a jestful hurt look and rubbing his shoulder. "She's always wanted me to play." Vanessa nodded along as if she was deeply familiar with the game.

"Perfect, we'll get it done," Steve said as he looked over his shoulder. "Oh wow, that was quick."

"Hey, you found some meat!" Dylan yelled as Jesse came back down the wooden stairs carrying a frost-covered ziplock bag.

"I found it covered in ice in the back of the freezer. It doesn't say what it is but I opened it and it looks safe," he called back as he got closer to the group. "I'm guessing it's deer or something."

"Grill's still hot, I'll toss it on," Steve said, getting up from his chair.

"Wait, you're going to eat that, even though you have no idea what it is?" Vanessa asked, jaw agape.

"Of course, I'll eat the mystery meat," Jesse said, smiling. "Looks just like some thick slices of beef anyways." He pulled the dark, frozen meat chunks from the bag with his bare hand.

Marissa stifled a gag. "It's black," she whispered to Eric, unable to look away from the suspicious protein.

He shrugged and looked at it curiously. "I'm sure it's fine. Hey, make sure you nuke that thing and kill off any bacteria."

"Will do! It's not like you haven't eaten worse," Steve laughed. Jesse just pointed at him and nodded in concession.

"I'm going to help Steve grill my mystery meat," Jesse said, skipping away. "But we should get the games going."

"Good call, I'll teach them the rules," Dylan said. He got up from his seat and walked to the nearby white table and began setting out cups. Eric got up and walked towards the table. Marissa crinkled her nose, taking one more look at the frost-covered, black meat that she knew couldn't be safe to eat.

"WHAT GAME ARE we playing?" Marissa asked.

"Chesties. Or I believe you called it titty pong."

"Yes!" Marissa shouted. "I've been meaning to teach Eric to play for years!"

"Well, it's a simple game, for those who don't know," Dylan explained. "And I have a feeling it might just be you that doesn't know." Him and Eric looked at each other and laughed.

"I guess so," Eric conceded. He glanced at the setup on the table, noticing a set of three cups in each corner, and one in the middle.

"It's simple," Dylan placed one last cup on the table. "Your goal is to bounce the ping pong ball off the table and your partner uses their chest to knock it into your cups. Both teams throw at the same time, and each time you make a cup the person next to you drinks and flips it. After you hit all your cups, you have to double-bounce that ball into the middle cup." Dylan finished his explanation and looked around.

"Makes sense to me," Eric said. "Is that how you used to play?" He looked at Marissa and Vanessa.

"Yep," she answered. "I'm so excited!"

"And the loser," Dylan added. "Has to shotgun a green snapper."

"What's a green snapper?" Marissa asked.

"Lose and you'll find out," Steve said, returning from the grill, a beer in hand. "So for teams I'm thinking," Steve paused and pointed at Eric and Marissa. "You two are a couple, right?"

"Yes," Marissa said with a smile and turned her head towards Eric. Dylan was walking around the table filling cups with beer.

"Cool, just making sure," Steve began again. "So you two will be partners, then I'll take Jesse so none of you have to deal with triple M."

"Triple M?" Marissa asked.

"Mystery Meat Man," Steve smiled as he answered. Everyone laughed.

"That leaves you and me," Dylan said to Vanessa. "Are you cool with that?"

"We're gonna kick some ass!" Vanessa shouted as she exploded out of her seat, fist raised in the air.

"You guys play first," Jesse spoke surprisingly clearly for having a mouth full of food.

"True," Steve added, looking between Jesse and the grill. "That way this one can get some much-needed food and I can clean up."

"You heard them," Vanessa said, cheerily. "Come take your beating."

"Oh, it's on," Marissa grinned as she lined up on the same end of the table as her sister.

"I guess that means I'm down here," Eric walked to the opposite end and stood next to Dylan. Dylan passed him a ping pong ball.

"Ready? Three, two, one, go!"

Dylan and Eric bounced their balls across the table towards the girls. Marissa was ready and the ball bounced off her chest and directly into a cup. Vanessa overestimated the bounceback of the ball and it dropped below the table. She quickly bent to pick it up.

Marissa slid the made cup over to her sister who immediately started drinking. Marissa bounced the ball back across towards Eric who leaned over the cups. The ball bounced off the string off his hoodie and dropped in front of the cups.

"Ahh, it hit my string!" he yelled, grabbing the ball and bouncing it back across as Vanessa finished her drink and expertly flipped it on the first try. Eric tucked the strings into his sweatshirt collar as Marissa knocked the ball in another cup and again passed it to her sister right after Vanessa bounced her ball across to Dylan.

Dylan dropped the ball perfectly off his chest but it thudded off the cup's rim. Marissa bounced hers to Eric who, without strings in the way, used his stomach as a backboard for the ball to bounce into his cup. Dylan quickly downed the cup but was struggling to flip it successfully. Vanessa again finished her drink and flipped her cup on the first try, but before Dylan could bounce the ball her way, Eric had bounced his and Marissa knocked the ball into her final cup.

"Ugh!" Vanessa exclaimed, grabbing the cup and chugging before her sister could even slide it over.

Marissa bounced the ball back to Eric, who again guided the ball successfully into his cup. He passed the cup to Dylan and threw it directly back to Marissa since she didn't have any more to make. She bounced the ball back and Eric barely touched it before it dropped into his last cup. Eric passed the last cup to Dylan, who had just flipped his previous cup successfully at almost the exact same moment Vanessa did the same on the opposite end.

Eric then lined up and tossed the ball towards the cup in the middle of the table with a precise amount of force. The ball bounced once, then twice, and hit the inside wall of the cup, dropping into the beer below.

"Yes!" Marissa and Eric screamed together, throwing their hands in the air.

"Come on, first try?" Dylan set down the cup, beer gone but no time to flip it.

"I like this game," Eric smiled, looking at Marissa's wide grin, then at Vanessa's salty smile of congratulations.

"We make a good team," Marissa met her boyfriend in the middle of the table for a quick kiss.

"You guys got waxed," Jesse laughed just before throwing the last giant bite of his mystery meat burger into his mouth. "Steve, let's go!" he tried to say but it came out jumbled along with some pieces of partially chewed bun.

"Coming!" He left the grill and jogged to the table. In moments, the beers were refilled and the game-faces were on.

"Ready? Three, two, one, go!"

"THAT'S SUCH A weird punishment," Marissa said after they were done, her face scrunched in empathetic disgust. Jesse slammed down his can of ginger ale and crushed it under his foot with triumph. Steve paused for a moment to shake his head with eyes slammed shut before continuing to gulp from the gash in the can.

"I don't get what's so bad about it," Vanessa shrugged as she reset the cups at one end of the table while Dylan mirrored her, all the while smiling and watching his friends chug their drinks.

"Ha you loser! Now you have to drink soda, fast!" Jesse said in a playful voice. His enjoyment seemed to overshadow the fact that this was a punishment. His partner finished his can with one last gulp before tossing it on the ground in front of him.

"Honestly, it sucks," Steve said with watering eyes. "It's all the worst parts about shotgunning. It's really cold and has lots of carbonation. But you don't even get the alcohol to feed your buzz."

"That's brutal," Eric said between laughs.

"Should we keep it going?" Dylan asked eagerly. "I'm not used to losing." He smiled playfully at Vanessa.

"Oh, so it's my fault?" she laughed back. "Let's switch up the teams and see what happens. Marissa, get over there." Marissa did as she was told and lined up diagonal from her sister.

"Guess it's you and me, Eric," Dylan walked over to Marissa's previous position.

"Let's do it," Eric smiled, looking at the concentrated faces of the girls at the table. "This should go pretty quick."

# CHAPTER 3

THE FIRE BURNED brightly as the flames cast moving shadows and crackled in the cool air. The wood pile was slightly depleted, the group's energy was moderately depleted, and the drink supply was almost entirely depleted.

"Anyone need a drink?" Jesse asked, walking ever so slanted to the cooler and opening it with a deep popping sound. He looked back as he bent into it and the rest of the group shook heads at him. Ice crashed in water as he extracted an amber bottle with an orange cap.

"Does anyone know any good ghost stories?" Vanessa said as the speaker in Steve's cupholder quieted down to change songs. She had her head on Dylan's shoulder and her hand on his chest while he had one strong arm around her keeping them from tipping out of the small, leaning lawn chair.

The group looked around at each other expectantly when Jesse sat down on his Adirondack chair and said, "I've got tons!" Then he tried to twist the cap off his bottle, failed, and stared hard at it. He then tried to open it by putting the lip on the edge of the wooden chair and bashing the top of the bottle. The only result was some small chip marks on the edge of the flat wooden arm. "Anyone have an opener?"

"I've got one," Marissa said, reaching into the front pocket of her jeans. Her car keys came out with a clang and she tossed them across the fire towards Jesse's outstretched hand. He missed the catch; the keys hit him in the chest with a sharp clatter causing him to wince.

"Thanks!" he said as he pulled them off his lap and fidgeted with what his squinting eyes perceived to be an extremely complicated and elaborate apparatus. He jingled the bright blue plastic feather on the key chain before noticing the metal ring with a flat internal edge.

"By the way," Vanessa giggled as she watched Jesse struggle with the simple bottle opener. "Who's Jeep is that out front?"

"It's mine!" Jesse looked up excitedly. "It's sweet, right?" He failed one more time with the bottle opener and Steve quickly grabbed it from him along with the bottle and popped it open, taking a heavy drink before passing it back. He looked at Eric and Marissa and rolled his eyes, head shaking with a smile.

"Just curious," Vanessa asked. "It is nice though."

"Thanks," Jesse grasped onto the bottle and opener and took a big swig. He fumbled his car keys out of his pocket, dropping them onto the ground below. He snatched them up aggressively, and then thrust them high for everyone to see. "Used to have a bottle opener myself but I broke it." He looked at the keys with a longing expression before leaning sideways and putting both sets into his side front jean pocket.

"Can't imagine how you broke it," Dylan said and winked at Vanessa.

"So, you guys wanted a story?" Marissa asked, eyebrows raised looking across the flickering flames to meet the eyes across the fire.

"You got one?" Steve asked, leaning forward in his lawn chair.

"I don't," she responded and then looked sidelong at Eric. "But I know someone that does." She patted him on the knee before getting up to grab another drink from the cooler. Eric watched her walk away and tucked his lips into his teeth.

"Ohhh, Eric's got the stories, does he?" Steve gave a devilish grin. "Come on then, give us one."

"I didn't plan on telling one," he put his hands up defensively. "But I suppose I could cook something up. Just give me a minute to think."

"Take your time."

Marissa came back with a beer can for herself and Eric. "Here," she said, giving him the icy drink. "To fuel creativity." She sat back down in the chair next to him and scooted it a little closer.

"Yeah, take your time," Jesse said with a slur as he stood up again from his Adirondack chair with a bit of a struggle. "That way I can go drain the snake." He stumbled away from the fire and towards the woods adjacent to the yard.

A moment passed as the group sat staring into the fire and Jesse continued away behind the cover of trees.

"I'll give it a shot," Eric said. "Should I wait for Jesse?"

"Definitely not," Dylan said. "He could be a while."

"Yeah, let's hear it," Vanessa added, snuggling up even more against Dylan.

Eric began the story, smiling as he stared into the flames before him. "There's another forest, similar to this one, just a few miles away. Much like tonight, the sun has gone down, and the warmth of the day has been traded for the cool breeze of the night. The moon is just a sliver in the sky overhead, and the stars are beginning to come out.

"Some people might notice that it's common to hear a crack in the woods while you sit by a fire. This isn't a random occurrence. It happens for a reason. Because out there in the dark, hidden by the swaying shadows of the trees, is the Chimerist.

"The Chimerist was once a scientist, working on new types of cures for diseases. Their goal was to combine the best features of different animals, since disease is much less common in animals than it is in humans. But when the Chimerist was trying to cure cancer, the other researchers wouldn't let them mix a pig with an alligator. They said it was unethical.

"Outraged by the lack of support, and driven out of the industry by people that thought they were crazy, the Chimerist went into a self-made exile in the woods. To do the real research they wanted, they built a cave system under the trees with a full laboratory. Now they can do all of the experiments they want and they are constantly creating new creatures by cutting them in pieces while they're alive and sewing their circulatory systems together. Then their blood pumps back and forth between both animals."

Vanessa clutched on to Dylan and made a fake puking sound. Eric continued with the story.

"Legend has it, the Chimerist is constantly seen in the woods with their half man, half alligator servant. This creature has both heads, and supposedly over time their minds have exchanged bits of their consciousnesses to become one.

"They say the creature has patches of human skin and scales all over its body, and can run as fast as a man but swim as fast as an alligator. This is useful for the Chimerist, because they are always trying to create new hybrids, and after these hybrids are tortured and accept their fates, they begin to work for the Chimerist to find new victims.

"Because the Chimerist's lab is underground in the forest, the people that get captured the most are those who sit around campfires in the dark, in excluded sections of the woods. They say that if you hear a crack in the woods, that's one of the Chimerist's hybrid scouts, getting ready to capture the first person to leave the comfort of the fire and walk into the woods."

Then suddenly there was a loud *crack* from the woods.

A creature strutted awkwardly toward them with a dark object in front of him. It curved in multiple directions, had several sharp points, and a blunt center. When it got closer to the fire, the object was held up to the group. "Hey guys," Jesse said, stumbling. His face now illuminated by the flames. "Look what I found."

"Horns?" Vanessa asked, taking a second to lean away from Dylan's shoulder and try to get a closer look.

"Antlers," Dylan whispered in her ear, just barely loud enough for the others to hear.

"Oh Antlers," Vanessa said innocently. "They looked like horns until he came closer to the fire." Marissa and Eric exchanged grins at her innocent and incompetent act. It wasn't the first time she acted helpless around an attractive man.

Jesse untied a short rope from one of the Yeti handles before slumping back down into his Adirondack chair. He began fidgeting with the rope and the antlers.

"What are you going to do with that?" Steve asked, voice agitated at Jesse's incoherence.

"You'll see," he said as he started wrapping the rope around and around the antlers.

"I guess the Chimerist created a human-deer hybrid too." There were uncomfortable chuckles around the fire. "Should I get back to it?" Eric asked loudly. There were murmurs of assent. "Some nights you might hear the whistle of the wind and wonder why it's making such a shrill sound. But it's not the wind at all. No, it's the victims of the Chimerist, screaming as they suffer in the underground cave laboratory.

"They say there was one person to escape experimentation. That person was said to have been combined with three house cats. If you ever look into the darkness, and really focus, you might see its three sets of glowing eyes. You might hear its shrill, tortured cries as what was once a human and three cats has come to accept itself as a monster. Now, its sole purpose is to scare people away from the forest, to prevent the Chimerist and their monsters from finding more victims."

There was silence around the fire. Then suddenly...

"What the hell, dude?" Steve said. "You just came up with that?"

"Yeah," Eric said simply, almost guiltily.

"What the hell is going on in your head? You know we have to sleep tonight, right? Damn that shit was existential." Steve's eyes were somehow both bulged and narrowed while his mouth hung agape.

"It was a good story," Dylan laughed.

"I liked it too," Vanessa said. "Especially the cat-person."

"I have to pee," Jesse stood abruptly and jogged while leaning at an angle towards the woods. His new antlers stayed firmly attached to his head as he ran but the weight pushed his neck forward ever so slightly-a strange, sudden deformity.

"Well, now that I'm thoroughly creeped out, I think I'm going to head inside and go to bed." Dylan had to wait for Vanessa to get off of him before he could stand himself. The chair looked almost relieved after the two bodies were off it.

"Yeah, it is getting late," Steve added. "And we've got a full weekend ahead. Can't let night one get too out of hand." He stood from his seat and quickly packed the leftover food wrappers and beers into the cooler, which he then lifted to head inside. "See you all tomorrow." Dylan began following close behind.

"Wait, what about Jesse?" Vanessa asked, looking into the darkness of the woods.

Dylan called out. "Jesse, you good?" His voice carried into the forest.

A winded shout came from the shadows. "Yeah, I'm… agh." The harsh sound of vomiting came hacking back toward them, followed by the sound of thick liquid splashing against dry leaves.

"We'll see you inside then?" Dylan called again. The choking sounds died down.

"Yeah, I'll be there in a minute… agh." And the disgusting noises continued

"Well as fun as it is to listen to that," Eric pointed towards the woods. "We do have a hike planned in the morning." Vanessa frowned and wrinkled her nose as Eric and Marissa both got up and began packing their own things. Then suddenly Vanessa's eyes widened and she had a smile on her face.

"Hey Dylan," she called out. "What's your side of the cabin look like?"

"Uhh," came a confused response.

"Can you show me around?" she said as she started half walking half jogging toward him. He was almost up the steps and in the back door.

"Whatever you want," Dylan paused at the top of the steps and waited for Vanessa to scramble up the steps behind him. She slipped on a step, tripping on her long sweatpants, but Dylan pretended not to notice.

Eric and Marissa watched them venture inside, while hearing Jesse cough and spit in the woods. "She killed two birds with one stone," Marissa said, scrunching her nose at the distant sounds.

"What do you mean?" Eric cocked his head at her, his own face contorted in disgust.

"Well she's going to continue to hang out with the guy she thinks is attractive, for one. And she's going to use that as an excuse to not go hiking with us in the morning."

"Probably won't be using those bunk beds, huh," Eric added.

"Probably not," Marissa agreed.

"Well, shall we head in?"

"Of course," Marissa smiled and led the way as Eric followed with the mostly empty cooler.

"Don't stay out too late, Jesse," Eric shouted into the darkness as walked up the steps with hollow thuds at each footfall. He took one last look into the woods, wondering if Jesse would make it inside tonight.

# CHAPTER 4

THE HEAVY WOODEN door creaked open abruptly. "Hey Dylan, have you seen Jesse?" Steve stood in the doorway as Dylan quickly threw the quilted comforter over Vanessa's half-naked body. "Shit, sorry guys."

Steve's eyes darted quickly between the two heads that were exposed above the blankets. "Maybe knock next time," Vanessa suggested, shaking her head in short quick movements.

"What's up with Jesse?" Dylan asked, holding the blanket on Vanessa while he sat up against the wooden slat headboard of the bed. His upper body glistened with sweat.

"I don't know," Steve answered, taking a couple of steps closer to the bed. "I haven't seen him this morning and he's not in his room."

"Did you hear him come in last night?" Steve shook his head.

"Did you check the bathroom?" Vanessa suggested. "He was puking his guts out last night."

"He's not in the bathroom. I checked out by the fire too but he's not there either. The Jeep's still here."

"Maybe he went for a morning walk through the woods," Vanessa said in an uninterested tone.

"Maybe," Dylan agreed, his eyes narrowed. "Maybe we should do the same. We might run into him."

"Good call," Steve added. "I'll throw on my boots and see you guys outside."

"Might be a couple minutes," Dylan said as Steve turned around to leave. Vanessa laughed as the blankets whooshed and Steve quickly closed the door behind him. He shivered and scrunched up his nose.

❖ ❖ ❖

"Are you still reading that weird mythology book?" Marissa asked. She sat in a sweatshirt and sweatpants near the window in a wooden rocking chair with a thin red cushion. Her legs were crossed and her tablet was folded in her lap.

"Yeah," Eric flipped a tannish-brown page. "It's really interesting. This Alan Roberson guy was really into Native American culture and folklore. The book is filled with his notes." He turned the book around and held it up to reveal old typed words and a few images on the pages, surrounded by black ink scribblings.

"Any good folklore?" Marissa smiled sarcastically as she uncrossed her legs and stood up to approach the neatly-made bed Eric was laying in.

"Are you bored or something?" Eric smiled back as she sat next to him, one leg dangling off the bed.

"Well we couldn't go on our hike," she said with a mixture of irritation and lightheartedness. "Shouldn't have given my keys to Jesse I guess."

"He probably could've gone with a few less beers," Eric agreed. "Maybe once everyone is up and out today we'll grab them and just do the hike tomorrow before we head home."

"That's what I was thinking too," Marissa said. "But we'll have to convince Ness too, and you know that's not going to be easy."

"We're driving, right? Do we have to give her a choice?"

"I guess not. But I don't want her to be more pissed off than she usually is in the morning. That girl needs at least four coffees before she can even tolerate a conversation with anyone."

"Anyone she's not sleeping with," Eric mumbled just loud enough for Marissa to hear.

"Hey, she's still my sister," Marissa gave Eric's thigh a light smack. Eric responded by smiling and giving Marissa the big eyes. She met his playful gaze. "Yeah, yeah, yeah I know. You're not wrong."

Eric laughed as he turned another page of the book. "Read me something interesting," Marissa changed the subject as she saw a black and white image in the book.

"Memegwesi," Eric read aloud. "Memegwesi are small spirits that spend their time near riverbanks. They were originally created from the bark of trees and are about the size of a child. They have large heads, narrow faces, and whether or not they have a nose depends on the region in which they are found, or according to other theories, the type of bark from which they were made. They are extremely hairy over their hard, cracked skin. You may hear their voices and mistake them for the whine of a dragonfly."

"The whine of a dragonfly?" Marissa squinted. "What does that even sound like?"

"Bzzzzmer," Eric made a high-pitched noise demonstrating his approximation of the noise in his imagination. Marissa laughed and smacked him on the leg again.

"Should I keep going?" Marissa gestured assent with a flick of her hand.

"Should you come across a Memegwesi, show respect and you have nothing to fear. While typically only visible to children and healers, there have been exceptions. Look out for their symbol-carved rocks by the riverbank and be sure not to disturb their stone canoes. They are generally good-natured and helpful spirits, though they enjoy some good trickery now and then." Eric finished reading.

"That was definitely…" Marissa paused. "Interesting." Eric smiled at her before pointing some scribbled words on the page's margin.

"Check this out," he said. "Alan has some notes. 'Those damn Mems. This morning when I was fishing from my kayak I got dragged against the current. Don't know how it's possible but I had a time getting back. Only reason I stopped going upstream was because I got stuck in a thick section of reeds near the bank. It was lucky though. Caught more bluegill in an hour than in the last three weeks combined. Can't tell if these Mems are pranking me or helping me.'"

"So this Alan guy is off his rocker or what?" Marissa asked.

"He wouldn't be the first writer that's a little crazy," Eric said. "Wait there's more. 'Tipped one of their stone canoes by accident today. Hopefully they're a forgiving bunch. I apologized but I can never tell if they're paying attention.'"

"Would a stone canoe even float?"

"I guess maybe it depends on the type of stone and the shape of the canoe. The Archimedes Principle," Eric answered, moving his hands in circles in front of him.

"Okay nerd," Marissa chided.

"Hey!" Eric said defensively.

Marissa leaned over and kissed him on the cheek. "It's okay, you're my nerd."

Suddenly there was a knock on the door. "Riss! Eric! Are you in there?" It was Vanessa shouting urgently through the bedroom door.

"Yeah, Ness," Marissa answered. "What's up?" Vanessa opened the door quickly and her eyes were wide. Dylan and Steve both stood behind her with concerned expressions.

"We can't find Jesse," Dylan answered from behind Vanessa. "He's been gone all morning and..." He trailed off. Vanessa turned back to look at him with a worried frown.

Steve took half a step forward. "But we found blood."

THE GROUP OF five walked through the woods a stone's throw from the backyard. Their footsteps crunched and sometimes squeaked as they passed through the decaying and sometimes freshly fallen autumn leaves. The leaves covered almost every inch of the forest floor, making it difficult to avoid catching shoes and boots on the occasional hidden root or broken branch.

Steve put his hand against the rough, vertically-ridged trunk of a red oak. "It's right over here," he said, slowing to let the others catch up. At the foot of another red oak the leaves were scattered, revealing an almost scratched looking underbrush of dirt, grass, and clovers. Between the tree and the patch of exposed earth, there was something else.

Eric squinted as he looked in front of him, hesitating to step closer. After a moment of looking he used his hand to plug his nose. The air reeked. It smelled like stale, rotting meat, mixed with flat beer and vodka.

Marissa stepped past Eric, her nose scrunched slightly. "It definitely looks like Jesse was here last night. I hope he's okay." She hesitantly crouched down to look at the mess at the base of the tree. It was a splattering of extraordinary volume, looking solid in some areas and liquid in others. The majority was a dull yellow in color, with some brown flakes dotting the denser sections. Then she saw the wine-red pool underneath it all. There were some red streaks on top of the pile, but the dark puddle seemed to surround the massive chunks and flowing rivers of day-old vomit. "That's a lot of blood," she murmured.

Eric came up next to her, still covering his nose. "There's more over there," he pointed from the pile at the base of the oak to a yellow birch a few strides to the side. Steve and Dylan walked up behind Eric and looked towards the other tree.

"Oh shit," Steve said. Dylan was already moving towards the birch where there was a reddish-brown stain in the shape of a hand on the trunk. Vanessa gasped as she finally got the courage to look at the new spot.

Dylan stumbled, nearly falling onto the leaves when he was a few steps shy of the tree. "What the..." He bent down and felt through the leaves beneath him. He grabbed something and began pulling it off the ground, stepping back as if he stood on part of the object. Dylan's head tilted and his eyes narrowed as he looked back at the others.

"Oh shit," Steve said again.

Eric and Marissa looked at each other with wide eyes. Vanessa took half a step back and tripped on a root, exclaiming terrified profanities as she fell.

Dylan scrunched up the tattered, blood and vomit stained, flannel shirt in his hands. Eric walked up next to him to look at the stained birch tree and examine the surroundings.

"I don't see any more blood," Dylan said, looking around. The two continued to look around but after a few moments they found nothing new.

Marissa walked back to Vanessa, who was still brushing off her clothes from her fall. She had a few tears running slowly down her face that she tried to wipe away with her shoulder. "Are you okay?" Marissa asked her.

"No," Vanessa grumbled. "Jesse is missing and we found blood and his shirt, so that's not good." She explained what was already clear to everyone. "So he's probably hurt somewhere and it's going to get dark in a couple hours."

"I know," Marissa agreed. "But we'll figure it out." She tried to be encouraging and put her hand on her sister's shoulder.

"What..." Vanessa was taking short, unsteady breaths. "What are we going to do?"

"We just have to stay calm," Marissa said steadily, appearing more calm than she felt. "We'll get help."

"How?" Vanessa shrugged the hand off. "We can't call anyone, remember? Who's going to know we need help? We're out here in the middle of nowhere!" Her voice was elevated now, approaching hysteria.

"We'll drive into town," Dylan said confidently. "We'll go to the police station and explain that our friend is missing and they'll send out a search party."

"We can't," Eric said quietly, looking at Dylan.

Dylan's face twisted with confusion. "What do you mean? You guys have a car, right?"

Eric closed his eyes and shook his head. "Jesse has our keys."

"What!?" Vanessa yelped, stumbling again but quickly regaining her balance.

Dylan's head dropped. "He needed your bottle opener," he realized, feeling defeated.

Steve had been silently listening as his eyebrows rose higher and higher as he processed the situation. "Oh shit!"

# CHAPTER 5

STEVE AND DYLAN tossed more logs onto the fire. It was now burning steadily but their job wasn't done just yet. They turned around to get another load.

"Are you guys sure this is a good idea?" Vanessa asked, sitting in a lawn chair near the growing flames. She sat holding her knees to her chest, chair moved so that the armrest overlapped with Marissa's.

"I think we're open to any other suggestions," Dylan grunted as Steve stacked log after log in his arms.

"If Jesse is lost out there in the woods somewhere, he'll see the fire and find his way back. Seems like a reasonable plan to me." Steve finished stacking wood into Dylan's arms and began to grab a few logs of his own. "Honestly, he probably did get lost but knowing him he found some other cabin and made friends with people there. Then he'll stroll back in the morning like nothing happened, telling us all about the awesome people that live across the lake."

Eric and Marissa exchanged doubtful looks. "Also," Eric decided to contribute. "If he is still lost in the woods, the good thing is that it's really not that cold out tonight so if he doesn't see the fire he should be fine staying wherever he is for now. We can hike into town tomorrow and get help."

"Exactly," Steve said optimistically.

Vanessa had a doubtful expression of her own as she looked between Eric and Steve. "Aren't there animals out there? What if he got attacked by one and that's why we saw the blood?"

"I think the blood was probably just from puking. Sometimes that happens if you tear your stomach up enough," Marissa answered.

"Still though, what if it wasn't?" Her gaze found Eric's eyes and stayed there.

Eric hesitated, looking up for the answer. "There aren't any wolves. But there are probably coyotes, foxes, maybe the occasional black bear. I wouldn't worry too much about those." His words antagonized his true thoughts.

"I think all of those are pretty scared of humans too," Steve added as he got near the fire again and tossed on his logs with a crash of sparks and smoke. Then he began unloading the logs in Dylan's arms and setting them next to the firepit.

"That's not ideal," Vanessa muttered, keeping her voice low so she wouldn't damage Steve's optimistic mood.

"Don't forget about the Memegwesi," Marissa added with a subtle smile, attempting to lighten the mood.

"The mem what?" Dylan asked, finally unburdened from the weight he had been carrying.

"Memegwesi," Eric answered. "She was making a joke about a Native American folklore book I found at the house."

"Well let's hear it," Dylan said as he took a seat in one of the Adirondack chairs around the fire. Steve followed suit.

"Sure, maybe it'll lighten the mood a bit," Eric said, sitting forward in his lawn chair. "Memegwesi are basically these little, hairy spirits that live on the edge of the water. Apparently they're made out of tree bark, and love to pull lighthearted pranks. The guy who owns this place," he gestured at the cabin. "Thinks they're real."

"Are they like ghosts that haunt him or what?" Steve asked.

"No," Eric shook his head. "Supposedly they're benevolent spirits that love pranks."

"Pranks?" Dylan questioned, a smile creeping onto his face.

"Yeah," Eric chuckled. "The guy thinks that they pull his kayak around in the water while he's fishing. He thinks they make it harder for him to paddle back to the dock."

"But also," Marissa encouraged him to continue.

"But also, he said the place he got dragged to was the best fishing he'd ever had," Eric finished.

"So they're helpful little hair people," Vanessa concluded, skepticism obvious in her expression.

"That's what the book says, and Alan Roberson claims they're real in a bunch of different notes in the book."

"He's the guy who wrote the book?" Dylan asked.

"No," Eric answered. "He is an author though. But this book is a collection of Native American folklore by a different author. Alan just loves writing his own thoughts and experiences in the margin."

"Book vandalism," Dylan said. "Not a fan of that." Eric nodded and smiled in agreement.

"Well maybe these little hairy spirits will help Jesse find his way back," Steve said, holding his palms up with outstretched arms as if talking to the heavens. "Dear Memgesis."

"Memegwesi," Marissa corrected. "Is that plural?" She looked at Eric. He shrugged.

"Dear Memegwesi," Steve repeated, ignoring the question. "Please guide our friend Jesse and protect him on his travels back here to us."

It was just then, sitting around the fire, that there was a strange sound that could only be described as the whine of a dragonfly.

THE GROUP SAT around chatting for a while. Steve and Dylan told stories about Jesse, causing laughter and smiling all around the fire. There was suddenly a moment of silence.

A sharp rustling of leaves interrupted the moment. Eric, Marissa, and Vanessa glanced to their right towards the woods while Dylan glanced left from across the fire. Steve had to crane his neck to look over his shoulder into the darkness behind him.

"Wait," Steve leaned towards the woods and narrowed his eyes. "I think I see…"

There was more rustling and the snap of a twig.

"Jesse!" Steve shouted. "It's Jesse," he said back to the group before getting out of his chair. "I just saw his face through the trees!"

Relief washed over the rest of the group as Steve began sprinting into the woods to retrieve their lost friend. "Jesse, we're over here!" Steve yelled while waving his hand and sprinting into the darkness of the trees beyond. "Jesse!" his voice called one more time but much quieter now.

The rest of the group around the fire stood, except for Vanessa who remained frozen, hugging her knees in the lawn chair. They all looked to the woods eagerly.

"Did you get him?" Dylan called out to Steve, who was nowhere to be seen.

There was no answer.

"Steve!" Dylan shouted again, inching towards the edge of the dark woods. He pulled out his phone and turned on the flashlight, barely illuminating a few feet in front of him.

"Do you see him?" Eric asked, walking up behind Dylan and taking his own phone out to add to the small but comforting bubble of light.

"No," Dylan responded in little more than a whisper. His heart was beating rapidly, and his breaths were haggard. He forced air into his nose and out of his mouth.

*Snap!*

Both of them jumped as a branch alarmingly close to them snapped. The wind rustled and the sounds of moving leaves seemed to pick up, though there was rustling and unsteady crunching coming from the dark forest ahead.

Dylan took one more deep breath, steadying himself. "That's it. I'm going after him."

He turned to Eric with worried eyes and Eric gently nodded. "I'll come too."

The two began stepping cautiously past the tree line that separated the yard from the forest. Civilization from the wild. Known from the unknown.

"Wait up!" Marissa called, jogging from the fire towards the woods. Neither Dylan nor Eric heard her call out as they proceeded into the darkness, disappearing.

"Riss!" Vanessa called before her sister reached the edge of the yard. "Don't leave me here alone!" Vanessa stood up now, desperately looking to her sister and taking half a step towards her. In her step she felt the heat of the fire. The safety it provided.

"I'll be right back!" Marissa yelled without looking back and vanished beyond the trees. Vanessa was stuck by the fire, immobilized as the cool wind began screaming all around her. She pulled her chair inches from the edge of the fire, grabbing an unburned log to hold while she sat back down. If anything came here, she would be ready. Hopefully.

Vanessa looked into the woods, scanning for any sign of her sister. Or Dylan. Or even Eric. They were all gone.

She strained her neck, trying to listen but she only heard the cracking fire, and the gentle movement of the lake pushing against the dock behind her. A gentle breeze pushed sparks from the fire, causing her to flinch.

*CLUNK!*

Vanessa spun around, knocking her chair over as she hefted her log. It sounded as if someone threw a heavy stone into the water from the dock. She breathed fast, wide eyes scanning the shoreline.

In the faint firelight she could see little circular ripples, expanding from one spot in the water. Where the stone must've hit.

"Please come back," Vanessa whimpered as she stood still as a statue, watching everything around her without moving her head. She pleaded to a higher power for the return of her sister. She hoped they would see each other again.

DYLAN'S FOOTSTEPS GREW more confident with each stride in the darkness. "Where could he have gone?" He murmured, more to himself than to Eric, who walked a few steps to his right.

"I have no idea," Eric responded, crunching dry leaves as he lit tree after tree with his phone's flashlight. They walked in silence for a moment, attempting to study their concealed surroundings. It was deathly quiet, other than their footsteps and the brushing of leaves in the wind.

"Hey!" Marissa whispered from behind. Eric snapped around as Dylan maintained a steady pace forward.

"What are you doing?" Eric asked, heart racing. The light from Marissa's phone shone directly into his eyes until he put his hand on it and lowered it slightly.

"I came to help look," she replied, still whispering. Eric looked behind her and saw nothing. He wasn't sure how far they were into the forest and it made his heart beat even faster. It was like being on a boat with no land in sight.

"Okay," he said. "Just stay close to me, alright?" She nodded and grabbed his hand in the darkness. Together they turned around to continue the search. Dylan's light was far ahead now. Eric's strides lengthened to catch up and Marissa's shorter steps accelerated to keep up.

"Dylan," Eric called in a moderate volume. There was no response, but he noticed that the flashlight wasn't moving anymore. It floated several yards in front of them, but Eric and Marissa were getting close. Soon they could see Dylan's silhouette, standing even more still than the nearby trees in the wind. "Dylan," Eric whispered this time.

Suddenly Dylan's head turned to look at them, and tears were streaking down his face. He looked like he was weeping but made no sound. Slowly his free hand began to rise up, shaking in front of him and he pointed in the direction of his flashlight. Eric furrowed his brow, but then followed the gesture with his own flashlight and eyes.

Marissa was slightly behind Eric, still staring at Dylan, not daring to say anything. She held Eric's hand and waited as Dylan's gaze left them and refocused on the illuminated scene ahead.

Eric froze. His blood ran cold and his hands started to drip sweat. His grip on Marissa's hand tightened, but he didn't dare move. He stood, motionless, trying to comprehend the image before him. The light barely reached, but shadows told the story.

There, in the dark was a creature crouched on the ground. Its narrow frame came straight up as it sat on unseen legs. The animal's spine and ribs jutted out sharply from pale gray flesh that was slashed with shallow cuts and stained with dirt. The head and arms were concealed by its slender body which bobbed up and down irregularly, facing away from the three terrified onlookers.

Only once their eyes had processed the nightmare before them could their ears and noses begin to function again. They heard squishing and tearing coming from the creature. Its breath was ragged and shallow, with deep, animal-like grunts seeming to reverberate from deep within the emaciated body.

Then the smell took hold. Desensitized to the comforting smells of forest and soil around them, the three were hit with a pungent, nose-curling stink. It was the smell of feces. It was the smell of uncontrolled mildew. It was the smell of putrid, rotting flesh.

Marissa had to smother her gasp with her sleeve as tears began streaming silently down her face. Dylan remained motionless, eyes now closed as he hyperventilated. Eric's jaw dropped as he ventured a subtle movement of his light.

To the monstrosity's side was a familiar face. Steve's eyes looked back at the three, unmoving and lifeless. His face was pale, with blood dripping out of the corner of his mouth. His blond hair stained with red. His body was the object of the creature's obsession.

Marissa almost fell as she instinctively leaned back but Eric was quick to help her regain her balance without causing too much of a disturbance. He held her and wordlessly pointed back the way they came, putting a finger to his lips. Marissa turned, but before she could move Eric put a soft hand on Dylan's shoulder.

"Ahh!" His tear-filled eyes sprang open in surprise and looked in all directions. His presence seemed to shrink down from his large frame into just a shell of who he once was. He dropped his phone and sprinted off into the woods, crunching leaves and sticks alike in a crash of panicked noise.

Eric held his breath, and watched Dylan run, not daring to make a sound. He turned to look back at the creature who stopped the gasping and swallowing they heard before. The creature now looked to the left, in Dylan's direction.

Marissa stayed still, facing away while Eric caught a glimpse of the animal's head for the first time. Spikes jutted out in several directions from the head. The spikes were a couple feet wide, and spread out nearly symmetrically from the center of the scalp.

Then suddenly it began to stand, still looking off into the darkness that consumed Dylan. Its body cracked with every bony movement as it grew gradually taller. It leaned back off of its front legs and took a staggering, impossibly balanced posture on its hind legs. The slender frame elongated, stretching skin over sharp bones almost to the point of tearing. The front legs now hung at its sides revealing long, human-like hands.

"Weee-ee-end!" The monster shrieked as its entire body cracked like bones and rusty hinges. It took off in a sudden sprint, alternating between running on two or four legs, it quickly vanished into the darkness after Dylan.

"Weee-grrr-ack!" Another shriek cut through the night and transformed into a guttural, animalistic growling.

"Go!" Eric whispered, gripping Marissa's hand tighter as they ran, phone flashlights illuminating the dark forest. Every few strides one of them would stumble on a root or branch and be dragged back up by the other as they fled.

The fire was soon in sight. Eric and Marissa cleared the trees and entered the yard.

"Ahhhh!" Vanessa screamed as she stood from her chair ready to swing a piece of firewood.

"Ness, inside quick," was all Marissa could get out between breaths. Eric let go of Marissa's hand and grabbed the firewood, tossed it into the firepit, and shepherded Vanessa towards the cabin.

Footsteps rapidly approached from the woods. "Run!" Dylan screamed as he sprinted full speed into the yard and started towards the cabin. Marissa was up the stairs and inside first, followed closely behind by a terrified and confused Vanessa. Eric was right on their heels panting hard when there was a heavy slam on the steps beneath him. He turned back quickly, before continuing up the stairs.

"Go! Go! Go!" He shouted.

Dylan had slammed into the railing, but managed to scramble up, sprinting behind Eric. Blood streaked down his left forearm and right leg. His vision was clouded and he was dizzy, but he knew he had to get up the stairs. He caught up to Eric just as he was closing the door and slammed it back open before falling on the floor inside, smearing blood from his battered arm and knee onto the hardwood floor.

Eric slammed the door and locked the deadbolt and doorknob lock. As he turned from the door, Marissa and Vanessa came pushing the couch, scraping it loudly against the floor. Eric helped them shove it against the door and then collapsed on top of it.

"The front door!" Marissa yelled. She took off sprinting down the hallway. Moments later they heard the soft click of the lock, followed by the deep, satisfying thud of a deadbolt. Soon she came jogging back to the others in the space between the kitchen and the living room. Eric laid on the couch, panting heavily as sweat dripped down his frightened face. Vanessa stood, anxiously looking around her, still unsure of what just transpired.

"What the hell was that?" Dylan said as much to himself as the others around him. His wide eyes unfocused and his breathing ragged. Blood still dripped slowly down his forearm as he sat in a wooden chair with his elbows on his knees.

Marissa and Eric sat on the brown couch with their backs to the locked door. The two shared a terrified glance but neither spoke.

"Yeah," Vanessa began. She sat in a wooden chair pulled up close to her sister. "What did you guys see?" She wasn't sure she wanted the answer.

"Steve," Marissa mumbled, clenching at Eric's clammy, wet hand in between them on the couch.

"What about him?" Vanessa trembled but needed to know more.

Dylan put his hands in his face as a few wet drops fell to the floor beneath his knees. He began sobbing while shaking his head in his hands. "He's dead," he managed to get out between gasping cries.

Vanessa looked to Eric, who was steadying himself with long, deep breaths. Eventually he looked across Marissa and into Vanessa's concerned eyes. "There was an animal," he said, then pausing for a few more calming breaths. "It was eating him."

Suddenly Dylan jerked his head up, his voice cracking with hysteria. "That wasn't an animal! That was a monster! Have you ever seen something that looks like that? Because I haven't. Not in real life, not even in movies. It had horns and hands and I don't even know what! And it was eating Steve!" He stopped yelling for a moment before looking back down at the wooden floor. His voice lowered. "It was eating Steve."

His thousand-yard-stare returned as tears dripped silently down his face and his breathing returned to an uneven, almost hiccupping cadence.

Vanessa was crying now. There were no soft words of support. There was no speech for the dead. There was just a waking nightmare.

"It ran on four legs sometimes," Marissa spoke softly. "But then it stood on two. Almost like a…" She looked at Eric, a single wet streak on her face that she quickly wiped away.

Eric leaned forward and tilted his head. "Like a person?" He spoke the question but thought about the answer. "It can't be." He sat thinking to himself, eyes darting around the room as if he was looking around inside his brain for a solution.

"What can't be? What are you talking about, Eric?" Vanessa said, still recovering from Dylan's outburst and the contagious fear around them.

Marissa searched Eric's face for an answer but there was none to be found. He stood up suddenly.

"I'll be right back." He turned and gave Marissa a reassuring look before turning around again. He walked briskly past the kitchen on the right and the couchless living room on the left, down the hallway in between and rounded the corner at the end. There was a *thud, thud, thudding* of feet as he moved up the stairs to the master bedroom. Marissa and Vanessa looked up at the ceiling expectantly while Dylan remained staring into his abyss of shocked memory and thought.

Then the *thud, thud, thudding* returned as Eric descended the stairs and rounded the corner back into the hallway, approaching the couch rapidly. He sat back down on the couch and held a brown book out in front of him. It was *Algonquin Culture, Mythology, and Stories*.

He began quickly flipping page after page, paper whipping and cracking with each turn. "No, no, no," he commented while he moved through the book. Finally, he stopped and stared. "Here it is." Marissa and Vanessa both leaned closer to look.

*"Widjigo, commonly referred to as wendigo."* Eric read the heading and looked at the others.

"Oh my god," Marissa whispered, taking in the image on the right side of the page. "That's it."

"That's what you saw?!" Vanessa nearly yelled, breaths shortening with each intake of air.

Dylan sat up straighter, blinked rapidly, and then looked at the other three with a cocked head. Eric flipped the book around to face him and his eyes nearly went white as he gasped and jerked backwards, nearly tipping his chair over backwards but stumbling to catch himself.

"Why do you have that?" Dylan asked.

Eric snapped the book back around. "It was on the bookshelf," he answered. "It's where I got the story about the Memegwesi."

"Well, what's it say?" Marissa pointed at the text on the page.

"*Widjigo, commonly referred to as wendigo,*" Eric began, trying his hardest to read with even breaths rather than the panicked gasps he felt he needed. "The wendigo is a malevolent spirit that lives in the forest and is typically active in the Fall and Winter, and sometimes even the early Spring. No one knows where they go in the Summer. Wendigos are the personification of greed, showcasing its ugly nature and insatiable appetite. They are fearsome hunters that are both quick and strong.

"The characteristics of wendigos vary based on their origin, though they are commonly seen as gaunt, with icy or pale skin, in a form similar to a human. The skin is stretched across the prominent bones and deep within the sharp-ribbed chest is a heart encased in ice. Some wendigos have antlers, but this isn't universally true as it depends on the region as well as age of the spirit. Many have reported an overwhelming stench caused by their rotting flesh. Due to their insatiable nature, they can't get enough food to sustain them and their body may deteriorate over time. While they may resemble a human from afar, a close look at these spirits will give you all the warning you need. Should you come across a wendigo, your chances of survival are low. If you hear screams that sound like a mix between that of a human and a mournful animal, have no doubt, it is a wendigo on the prowl for its next meal."

"Okay, so we know what it is now," Vanessa interrupted. "But what do we do? There's still no phone service. No wifi. The driveway is like 15 freaking miles."

"Yeah," Dylan agreed, looking at Eric. "How do we kill it?"

"There's more here," Eric said defensively. "And there's a bunch of notes on the margins I'll need to try to read, but this guy's handwriting isn't the best."

"Keep going," Marissa encouraged, patting Eric on the leg with her hand while trying to read over his shoulder. Eric smiled and looked down again.

"There are several different beliefs about how wendigos are made. One or all may be correct, but they are as follows. One, acts of cannibalism can transform an individual into a wendigo. Two, a malevolent spirit may possess a vulnerable individual, likely someone who has succumbed to extreme acts of greed or selfishness. Three, wendigo psychosis is a medical condition which can cause altered perceptions of reality and a craving for human flesh. Wendigo psychosis is sometimes viewed as the beginning of the wendigo transformation as results of the two previously listed events. Oh, here we go," Eric said excitedly.

"Transformations are thought by some to be irreversible, though there have been claims to have saved souls and reverted them back to their previous selves. The only way to –"

*KNOCK! KNOCK! KNOCK!*

# CHAPTER 6

*KNOCK! KNOCK! KNOCK!*
The banging came again, hard on the front door.

"Are you guys in there?" a familiar voice came muffled through the closed door. Dylan jerked in surprise. Marissa and Eric stared at each other with wide eyes.

"Is that…" Vanessa started but was cut off.

"Hello?" the voice called out again.

"Hold on Jesse!" Dylan shouted, charging toward the door.

"Wait!" Eric yelled, standing and setting the book down. "What if it isn't him?"

"What do you mean 'what if it isn't him?'" Dylan snapped. Eric shrugged uncertainly.

"It's him," Dylan said with finality as he turned back toward the door and walked briskly down the hall. Vanessa scurried tentatively behind him like a puppy following its owner into the unknown.

"Do you smell that?" Vanessa asked, but Dylan ignored her, unlocking the door and thrusting it open.

"Weee-ee-ack!" A tortured, human-like shriek pierced their ears as the darkness between the doorframe filled with a gaunt figure. Gray-blue skin stretched across ribs and limbs and seemed to be peeling away on the joints. Its knees bent forward at an angle and its long arms sat at its side. The head was a silhouette in the darkness, facial features hidden but on top of its head were a wide, spiking rack of antlers. The stench of rotting flesh filled the cabin.

"What the..." Dylan began but then was silenced by a lightning-quick swipe of the creature's arm. Dylan flew back from the door and hit the side of the hallway. Vanessa jumped to the floor to reach for him. Eric took a few hesitant steps towards the door while Marissa stood up from the couch just behind him, her heart racing and knees trembling.

"Weee-grrr-end!" Another more guttural shriek came from the beast as it stepped quickly inside the door and in one motion scooped Vanessa off of Dylan.

"Ahhhh!" Vanessa screamed. "Help! Help!"

The emaciated creature held her effortlessly as she continued to cry out. It turned rapidly and strode back out of the open door.

"Riss! Help me, please!" she cried, high pitched panic taking hold as tears streamed down her face. The monster began to run on two legs, Vanessa's weight barely slowing it down as Eric sprinted to the door frame and watched it move away from the house and back towards the darkness of the forest.

"Ness!" Marissa was finally able to choke out, almost inaudibly. She was just behind Eric now, and he quickly spun around. Her eyes were both wide, vacant, and fixed on the darkness. Shock had already taken hold.

"Look at me, Marissa," Eric gripped her shoulders hard and leaned down to meet her gaze. "Look at me." Her eyes finally met his. "I'm going after her. Lock the door, then help Dylan. When I come back, make sure it's me. Do you understand?"

Marissa was shaking now, but she nodded. Eric quickly kissed her on the head, took a deep breath, and jogged out towards the darkness. Marissa steadied herself enough to grab the door and slam it shut, locking the deadbolt with a deep thud.

She leaned on the door and took three deep breaths. That's when she heard the gurgling.

Eric bolted toward the tree line, trying to keep his footsteps light despite his speed. He could still hear the creature running and Vanessa's desperate screams for help, but the sound was getting farther and farther away.

He had out his phone flashlight, but it was barely enough to cut through the overwhelming darkness in front of him. His heart thumped nearly out of his chest and he felt nauseous. Vanessa's cries were now inaudible but he could still hear the rustling of leaves as the monster moved swiftly through the woods.

Suddenly the noise stopped. The only thing Eric could hear was his own, quiet footsteps. And his heavy breathing, which he tried his hardest to silence. He slowed his pace, rounding trees and stepping over roots and fallen limbs. The ambient sounds of the forests seemed to shout at Eric, warning him of the danger ahead, yet he pushed on, determined to try to help Vanessa. The crickets were deafening in the quiet, accompanied only by the sound of the wind on rustling branches and leaves overhead.

His light caught on something white amidst the brown and tan leaves below. It was one of Vanessa's shoes. His mind raced, fighting his instinct to take off running in the opposite direction, he took another hesitant step. He didn't see any other signs of her, so he trudged on desperately.

Eric took a few more steps and then realized how cold it had become. The brisk air took bites at the skin of his nose and ears. His fingers began to quiver as his body started to shake. He was getting close to where he thought the creature stopped. Just a few more steps.

A sudden, sharp tearing sound cut through the forest. It came from a short distance in front of him.

He began to move his light. It shook from the cold. No, it shook from the fear burning in his head and chest. He lifted it up from the shoe towards the dark outline of a tree.

He paused, unable to continue for the briefest moment before he got the courage to tilt his shaking hand just a little more. There was Vanessa, sitting at the base of the tree.

MARISSA HELD A soaking towel to Dylan's neck. The previously white cotton was now a deep shade of red. Dylan's breathing was ragged and uneven. He shot small sputters of blood from his mouth when he found the strength to cough, however weak the exhalation was.

Marissa removed the towel from the wound to check on it. Dylan's eyes went impossibly wide as he struggled for breath. The gash in his throat was deep. Blood spurted out with the rhythm of his heartbeat. He was losing too much blood.

"Just hang on Dylan," Marissa said through tears as she wrung the blood out of the small towel and returned it with pressure to the open wound. Through the soaked cotton she could feel the small pressure coming from each squirt of blood.

Dylan's breathing was slowing and his eyes twitched back and forth. Soon the squirts of blood began to slow. He gave out another series of small, almost silent coughs, but never took another breath in. His chest, now covered in dark red liquid like much of the ground, stopped moving altogether. His mouth hung open now and his eyes stared past Marissa, into the world beyond.

THE MONSTER WAS nowhere in sight. Vanessa's eyes were open, but there was no life in them. She looked right through Eric as he took a few careful steps closer.

He examined her body, or what used to be her body. Her limbs were intact, but her midsection wasn't. It was eviscerated. Halfway up her torso was a horizontal gash that spilled out directly below, revealing mashed organs and intestines. Blood soaked through everywhere and filled what room had been vacated from her stomach cavity. Eric now noticed the small bits and pieces of loose flesh that had been ripped away from her body, along with pieces of ribs.

"Oh my god," was all Eric could whisper as tears began to stream down his face.

Suddenly there was a crack of a branch from behind the tree. Leaves rustled with distinct motion, nothing like the smooth cascading of sound that came with the wind.

"Weee-grrr-ack!" The thin, bony creature came out from behind the tree as Eric flinched his phone up into its face. Its yellowing teeth were framed by long, midnight-colored hair and a pale, gray-skinned face–a face Eric recognized.

"No!" Eric shouted as he turned and ran as fast as he could.

# CHAPTER 7

MARISSA STOOD OVER the stainless-steel kitchen sink, scrubbing frantically. She slammed her fist on the soap dispenser a few more times, catching the thick liquid before lathering it on her skin. The scalding water and soap were finally working. Pinkish-red liquid dripped from her hands and down into the drain below.

Finally, after what seemed like hours of effort, she dried her now clean hands on the pumpkin patterned kitchen towel that hung from the oven handle. She left the water running so the current could wash the remaining blood out of sight.

When she flipped the faucet handle down and stopped the flow of water, she stood still, looking at her reflection on the microwave's dark glass. She stared, and the image stared back at her. It didn't look like her. It looked like a scared child with wild hair, wild clothes, and wild eyes.

*BANG! BANG! BANG!*

"Marissa, let me in!" Eric's voice shouted, coming muffled through the front door.

"Eric?" Marissa answered as she bolted from the kitchen and down the hall. She forced herself to look away from Dylan's body while being careful not to slip in the dark pool of blood.

"Yes! Hurry up!" Eric yelled. Marissa reached out to unlock the door, then stopped.

She froze. "What's my middle name?"

"What?!" Eric shouted in confusion. "Just open the door!"

"You told me to make sure it's really you!" Marissa's heart raced at the prospect of someone, or rather something else being behind the door. "So what's my middle name?"

There was a pause. Marissa could hear panting behind the door. "Claire! Now open the door!"

She quickly undid the deadbolt and wrenched the door open. Eric nearly fell into the hallway but caught himself on the wall. Marissa slammed the door shut again and locked it with a deep thud. Eric leaned on the wall, gasping for breath with his head braced on his forearm.

He began to try to speak. "I couldn't..." he gasped, still filling his lungs. "Tell...if it...was behind me...or not." He stopped trying to speak and took several more deep breaths.

"You're safe now," Marissa whispered gently, rubbing his back. She winced, feeling a sudden wave of nausea as she noticed a lingering spot of blood between her middle and pointer fingers.

"Dylan?" Eric asked hopefully. He hadn't yet noticed the lifeless body laying against the wall just a few feet away.

"He's dead," Marissa answered. "His throat was cut open. He lost too much blood." She said it much more matter-of-factly than she would've thought possible. Dead bodies were becoming all too common tonight.

Eric made no effort to move or speak for a long moment. When he eventually leaned back from the wall and found his balance he stared first at Marissa, then at Dylan's body. The head was covered with a blood-soaked kitchen towel. Eric looked down at his shoes and saw that he was standing in a pool of dark blood that was seeping along the floor planks. His eyes closed. When they opened Marissa saw complete and utter despair.

"Vanessa?" she whispered the question she had been dreading.

Eric's face went completely blank. "I didn't see her when I got out there," he lied. "I followed for as long as I could but then I couldn't hear anything. Eventually I just had to stop. But I saw it." He paused, fighting back tears. He couldn't tell Marissa the truth–not now. They needed to focus on surviving this nightmare.

"So she got away?" Marissa's eyes lit up, but she felt worry all the way to her core.

"She might've," Eric said. "Maybe I distracted him and she found a place to hide."

"I hope so, but she's still out there in danger," Marissa stopped to think. "Wait, why did you just say 'him?'"

Eric avoided her gaze. "I need the book."

They made their way down the hall and back to the couch blocking the back door. Eric picked up the old book and sat. Marissa joined him. He flipped through and found the wendigo section.

He began to read. "Transformations are thought by some to be irreversible, though there are claims of having saved souls and reverted them back to their previous selves. The only way to kill a wendigo is with fire. Since their hearts are encased in ice, melting that ice is the only way to set the spirit free of its physical form. Some say this is possible without killing the host but most say otherwise."

"Okay, is it afraid of the sun or something like vampires?" Marissa asked. "That way we could just wait out the night and then go find Vanessa and then go to the police." Her tone was desperately hopeful.

Eric just shook his head. "It doesn't say anything here about that. I'll keep reading; there's not much left." He moved his finger down the page to find where he left off. "There are few known shamanic rituals capable of driving wendigos away, and those can only be performed by the most capable spiritual leaders." Eric stopped reading. "That's all it says."

"What about Alan's notes?" Marissa asked.

"His handwriting isn't the greatest but I'll read what I can." He squinted at the scribbling in the margin of the page. "I went to the Mahican reservation downstate and talked with the Shaman again. He knew about my land and rental property. He told me to be weary of the greed of the explorer–I think he meant the renters. But he taught me about wendigos. Apparently they can even mimic human voices. Terrifying stuff, really.

He said the only hope in escaping the insatiable monsters is to distract it with human meat. Yeah, human meat. He said if you can throw some human meat one way and run the other you just might buy yourself a few extra minutes."

Eric shuddered, a sudden, sick idea coming to him. He pushed it away and read on. "He gave me a parting gift when I left. Handed it to me in a brown, wax paper wrapping. I opened it up and it looked like venison. I said thank you but the Shaman stopped me and looked deep into my eyes. 'This is meant for protection,' he said. 'It's human meat.' I thanked him for his generosity and barely made it to my car before I started puking in the gravel lot.

"I didn't ask where he got it, but maybe I should've. I tossed it in the bottom of the deep freeze, God forbid I ever need it."

"Oh my God," Eric said. "The meat. It makes sense now!"

"What do you mean?" Marissa asked, confused.

"That's the mystery meat!" Eric exclaimed, more in terror than excitement.

"Jesse..." Marissa paused. "He ate the human meat?"

"Yes!"

"Oh my God. That's disgusting." Marissa looked at Eric, still not understanding his sudden realization.

"It's Jesse!" he said as if that explained everything. Marissa just looked at him confused. "Jesse ate the human meat. Earlier in the book it said cannibalism is one way that wendigos are created, right?"

"I guess," Marissa humored him. "Are you sure you believe that?"

"Think about it," Eric encouraged. Jesse ate the human meat and got sick then disappeared." Marissa nodded. "Then when we were at the fire after we found Jesse's blood and everything, Steve said he saw Jesse in the woods and ran off to get him. Maybe he actually did see Jesse.

"Then, when it knocked and Dylan recognized Jesse's voice, it turned out to be the wendigo." Eric paused, debating on how he should continue. "And when I was in the woods looking for Vanessa... I saw the wendigo. And it had Jesse's face." He went quiet now. Marissa looked away from him, recounting the same events. She thoughtfully pieced together each instance of fear and uncertainty. After taking a moment to think everything through she understood.

A day ago, she never would've believed it. None of it should be possible. Yet she saw the creature with her own eyes. Twice. She saw two people die. She saw her sister abducted, screaming for dear life. She hoped Vanessa found a way to safety.

"Steve and Dylan are dead. Ness is missing. And the wendigo is Jesse." Marissa looked at Eric for confirmation. He nodded guiltily. "So what do we do now?"

Eric's guilty conscience made way for new ideas. "The book pretty much says that we're screwed, but let's think for a minute." He paused and looked around the room, then back to the book.

"Didn't it say the only way to kill it is with fire?" Marissa asked.

"Yes," Eric confirmed, looking at his girlfriend and hoping for inspiration.

"So we have to figure out a way to light it on fire," she added. "Or else we try running up the driveway."

Eric knew the second option was hopeless. "We have to set it on fire."

"I might have an idea," Marissa said. Her face went pale as she suppressed a gag.

# CHAPTER 8

"GOD, I HOPE this works," Eric said as he looked out the back window. He and Marissa sat there on the back of the couch that they pushed slightly away from the door. They were overlooking the backyard and unlit firepit.

"It will," Marissa said with more confidence than she felt.

The firepit wasn't just empty ash and small pieces of charred wood like it had been a few minutes before. The two had worked quickly, making just one trip down and back up. Eric loaded wood in the firepit to create what looked like a miniature log cabin with a flat roof.

Meanwhile, Marissa dumped all of the cooking oil she could find onto the wood and throughout the firepit and its edges. Once they both were done, Marissa laid the final piece into place; the bait.

"Do you think we'll have to wait long?" Marissa asked, carefully holding two bottles with kitchen cloths sticking out of the top.

Eric kept his eyes on the firepit. "I'm not sure. I guess it depends on when it finishes its last meal."

Marissa shuddered thinking about when the wendigo, or Jesse, was devouring Steve's body earlier in the night. "It doesn't look like it was taking its time."

Eric turned to her and cocked his head. He opened his mouth but then shut it again once he realized what she meant. Now wasn't the time to tell her. She needed to focus.

A sudden rustling came from the woods. The squeaky crunch of slow, consistent footsteps cut through the air.

"It's coming," Eric whispered. Marissa quickly ran to the gas stove in the kitchen and ignited it. She came quickly and quietly back to Eric's side. The sound of footsteps continued.

A shadow appeared at the edge of the forest and stopped. It leaned its scrawny, dark figure forward and its face came into the faint house light.

Marissa gasped. "It is Jesse!" The thin face rotated, the antlers no longer just strapped to his head, but fused to his skull, moving in perfect, solid unison with the rest of his body.

Then he began walking slowly, carefully towards the firepit. His pale body seemed to have rotted further since Eric saw him barely an hour before in the woods. His ribs spiked out of his chest. His shoulder blades were knives, gnashing through the air with each arm swinging step. His legs were bent and bony beneath his ragged jeans. His feet were the elongated paws of a wolf, with razor-sharp nails at the end of each long toe. He crept forward, stalking his prey.

Marissa and Eric were speechless. They were both taking concentrated breaths, fully aware of what they must do as the wendigo approached the firepit.

The monster was getting closer and closer to the firepit. It seemed to sniff and make low growling sounds that Marissa could just barely hear. It moved quietly through the grass.

Without a sound it suddenly jumped from the grass and up onto the short, thin edge of the metal ring around the pit. With another quick motion it moved its feet carefully inside as it eyed the prize sitting on top of the miniature log cabin.

There, it found a leg and an arm, cut off just below the knee and elbow. Marissa had painstakingly sawed the limbs from Dylan's corpse with a long, serrated bread knife. She cried while she did it, knowing she was losing some of her humanity.

Eric had tried to make the cuts, but he had immediately retched. He tried again but couldn't keep from dry-heaving. Marissa had to take over; she had the stronger stomach.

"He would want us to," Eric reassured her as she cried and sawed through skin, muscle, and bone. He sat next to her, looking away while she went about the work.

She knew it had to be done. It was the most important part of the plan.

The wendigo began slowly reaching for the leg. Marissa sprinted to the stove with her bottles. She held the kitchen towel that acted as the wick of the first bottle into the flames underneath the burner grates. It quickly caught fire and she sprinted back, doing her best to keep her movement quiet.

Eric slid the window open with a muffled squeaking sound. The wendigo, gripping Dylan's severed leg, bit down rapidly into the cold, pale flesh like a human might eat a chicken drumstick.

"Quick," Marissa whispered, handing Eric the flaming bottle of rubbing alcohol. She moved back.

He wound up his arm and quickly launched the bottle out the window and towards the fire.

It hit the edge of the metal ring with a bang and exploded.

Marissa ran back to the kitchen with the other bottle.

"Wee-eee-end!" the monster shrieked, still clutching its half-eaten prize. It took half a step back and turned toward the explosion, then toward the house.

Marissa came back and pushed the second flaming bottle into Eric's hands. "Here!" she shouted.

Eric turned, took aim, and threw the second bottle.

"Wee-eee..." The shriek cut off as the second bottle hit its mark and exploded in a massive blast of light and debris. The wendigo was thrown onto its back. It quickly rolled and stood. The fire left smoldering red splotches throughout its exposed skin, but the monster didn't catch fire.

"Dammit!" Eric yelled just before Marissa slammed the window closed.

The wendigo snarled at the blazing firepit. It snapped its head towards the window. Its open, drooling mouth revealed blood-stained teeth, and its wide, manic eyes stared right at Eric and Marissa.

"Oh no," Eric said quietly.

"Wee-eee-end!" Eric and Marissa both flinched as the shriek pierced the air. When they looked down, it was gone.

There was a sudden rumbling and thudding. It was closing in.

"Quick!" Marissa shouted. "The couch!" She and Eric jumped away from the couch and began trying to replace it in front of the back door. While she pushed, Marissa saw the wendigo out of the corner of her eye. It was in a mad sprint on all fours coming up the stairs towards the door.

"Hurry!" she yelled again, her heart beat accelerating. Eric groaned as he shoved the couch farther.

*BANG!*

Wood splintered as the monster slammed through the locked door, tearing the lock mechanism from the doorframe. The body wedged halfway in, grinding to a halt against the warped frame.

"Wee-eee-end!" The animalistic wail again assaulted their ears. The wendigo backed away from the door slightly.

"Get the knife!" Eric yelled. Marissa was a step ahead of him as she came running back from the kitchen, holding the knife like a sword with two hands out in front of her.

Eric grabbed one of the nearby wooden chairs, lifting it by the back, ready to swing.

*BANG!*

The door slammed again, this time swinging clear of the frame. The top hinge broke off, leaving it hanging at a sideways angle not quite touching the ground.

"Weee-grrr-ack!"

The wendigo broke for Marissa on all fours. Eric swung the chair and knocked it off course as it slammed into the wall next to Marissa. She swiped at it with the knife, barely grazing its shoulder. Black ichor seeped out.

The monster recovered as Eric wound up for another swing but missed. Marissa backed away, closer to the back door and window. The wendigo turned around, arms swinging, regaining focus on Marissa.

She was slowly backing up against where the door used to be. She stumbled on the half-fallen, shattered door. The creature approached her slowly.

"No!" Eric shouted as he jumped between Marissa and the creature. He still held the chair by the back, now pointing all four legs towards the wendigo like a blunt, four-pointed spear.

The wendigo stopped. Jesse's face was disturbingly familiar, despite the monstrous, emaciated form of the evil spirit that possessed him.

"Back!" Eric yelled, heart thudding out of his chest. His brows were now dripping with sweat. Marissa stood behind him, breathing ragged breaths and peering over his shoulder with terror. She still held the knife up, but to Eric's side.

"Wee-eee-end!" The wendigo shrieked defiantly. It lowered its antlers and charged across the room. Its full force thudded into Eric's chair legs, catching its bony torso, arms stretching toward him. The blow sent Eric crashing against the window behind him, shattering glass and wood. Marissa was forced to the side, but made another swipe of her knife, barely catching one of the wendigo's hands.

Eric regained his balance and leaned into the chair, extending his arms to push the wendigo back. It howled with a deep, guttural noise.

"Weee-grr-ack!" The creature's scream was deafening, causing Eric and Marissa to wince.

It charged with one final push. Eric was moved backwards. The window behind him was gone and his balance was failing. The wendigo's long, thin arms reached around the seat of the chair towards him. One clawlike hand scraped his wrist as he struggled.

Marissa repeatedly jabbed into the creature's ribs. She screamed like a maniac, making incision after incision through the flaking, pale skin.

Eric groaned as he exchanged a quick glance with Marissa. Tears streamed down her face and he had a momentary flashback seeing Vanessa's eviscerated corpse in the woods. His focus snapped back as his wrist was again raked by the wendigo's claws.

"Ahhhh!" He shouted, releasing the chair and grabbing the creature's arms.

"Wee-ee…" the creature screamed with him as he leaned back.

"Eric! Eric!" the sounds came back muffled and slow as his vision cleared. His ears were ringing, his head throbbing. "Eric!" The shouting was louder now.

He saw Marissa's face, upside down. Her lips were moving, but the sound was delayed. Then it all came back.

"Eric!" Marissa shouted. "Get up! We have to go!"

He sat up from the grass, glancing at the shattered window above. Sprawled out on the chair and the grass next to him was the wendigo. It wasn't dead; its rib-spiked chest was heaving.

"Let's go!" Marissa shouted, dragging him to his feet. His eyes were still on the monster, but then he noticed a familiar blue plastic feather sticking out of the pocket of the creature's ragged jeans.

"Wait," he said, unnervingly calm. His head still throbbed, his back searing in pain, but he ambled one step closer.

He cried out as he bent down and grabbed at the blue feather with his left hand. He yanked, and just as it came free, his wrist was caught in a vice grip.

"Wee-eee-end!" The wendigo shrieked, leaning up and kicking the chair away. Its clawed hand gripped Eric's wrist, its sharp thumb nail grating down to the bone.

"Ahhh!" Eric screamed out in pain.

"Eric!" Marissa cried. Eric forced himself to bend further, toward the monster. His right hand found his left and one grip loosened while the other took hold. He screamed, then threw his right hand over his shoulder. The car keys flew through the air, landing with a soft clang in the grass near Marissa.

Marissa was frozen as the wendigo stood, yanking Eric up with it.

"Ahhh! Riss! Go!" Eric shouted, punching the monster in the head. It shrieked, bringing its other arm up—an arm that had snapped during the fall and now dangled, uselessly.

"Wee-grr-ack!" the wendigo screamed, looking from its mangled arm back to Eric.

Marissa forced herself to look away, stooped, and picked up the keys. She fingered them fearfully and took two steps back.

"Go!" Eric turned his head towards her, eyes wide with fear. The veins on his neck surging with blood. He couldn't free his wrist; it was sliced halfway to his elbow. "Please Go!" Tears streamed down his face. He threw another punch with little effect. The creature barely reacted. He kicked at its legs with no result. Then he leaned back with all of his weight. It had no choice but to stumble forward with him.

Marissa looked at Eric, accepting his fate. "I'll come back with help." She said, not even sure if she believed herself. She continued backing away, wishing for some way to save him.

Then she felt heat against her face. The fire was still blazing. She looked from the flames to Eric's struggle with the wendigo and back. "The fire!" she yelled to him, voice cracking.

Eric glanced over his shoulder. The wendigo's head moved closer, mouth opening wide. "Go!" he shouted again just before the wendigo bit down hard on his wrist. "Aghhh!"

The sharp teeth pierced skin and snapped bone. The monster lifted its head slowly, excruciatingly tearing the flesh. Eric groaned, went pale, but retained his focus. He leaned back hard again, bringing both him and the wendigo closer to the firepit. It was only a few steps away now.

"Eric," Marissa called out, halfheartedly. She was still backing away. She moved towards the woods as she began to think about her sister.

Eric leaned with two strong, jerky movements. His heel hit the metal ring, and flames began licking at his shirt. His ruptured arm was still held by the wendigo.

Then Eric grabbed the wendigo's antlers with his good hand and gave a final backwards lean, throwing all of their weight toward the fire.

"Wee-eee-end!" They both fell into the flames, shooting up sparks and fiery debris.

Marissa turned and started running toward the trees. Her vision was distorted by salty tears, and she was whimpering, stumbling more from fear than injury.

"Noo!" Eric screamed. He and the wendigo struggled on their knees in the fire. "No! She's dead! Ahhhhh!"

Marissa turned back. Her stomach dropped, her hands shaking. The screaming and the screeching became distant. Eric was wrestling the monster in the firepit. The wendigo's skin was dripping; Eric's own skin began to warp and change. They slammed down again, sending sparks flying. Both of their mouths moved, eyes wide, making no sounds.

Marissa turned away. She didn't look back into the woods for Vanessa. She looked down at the keys in her trembling hand, then sprinted around the house and toward the car.

She unlocked it with a beep and slammed the door open, climbing in. Her right hand shook too violently to insert the key; she had to steady it with her left. She turned the ignition, and after a few whirs of the motor, the engine started.

Marissa slammed on the brake, pulled the car into reverse, and punched the gas pedal. She swerved, shifted into drive, and started speeding down the long, dark dirt driveway.

# EPILOGUE

ALAN ROBERSON STARED into the charred firepit. Inside the metal ring, two sets of bones lay mixed together, blackened with soot as if they had been roasted alive while fighting in the flames. He poked his rubber-capped cane through the ashes.

Lifting his cane, Alan held a dark set of antlers fused to a human skull. The sight made him shiver, pulling his mind back to the police station, and the poor girl who had endured it all.

He set down the skull and continued to pick through the ashen remains, causing small puffs of soot to shoot in the air. He hit something solid and rounded. Digging with his cane, he revealed a matte-black object, which tilted and rolled slightly down a hill of ash.

"Could it really be?" Alan muttered to himself, stooping to peer through his thin-framed glasses at the object. He began reaching toward it when he was interrupted.

"Well, she didn't lie about one thing." The disconcerted-looking police officer walked up behind Alan as he turned. "We found a body in the house. Two more in the woods. All of 'em in rough shape. Honestly, I've never seen anything quite like it."

"Hmm," Alan grunted, thoughtfully.

"Anyway, we won't know for sure what happened to them until the coroner gets here. He should be here soon." Alan nodded, the officer nodding in kind before walking back towards the house and driveway. Alan watched him go, seeing the red and blue lights flickering off the house and the trees at the edge of the woods. When the officer was out of sight, he returned his attention to the firepit.

He leaned into the metal ring and retrieved the black, fist-sized object. It was instantly cold in his hand. As he wiped away the soot, he felt a faint, terrifying vibration.

*LUB DUB, LUB DUB, LUB.*

Alan shuddered, nearly dropping the frozen heart back into the fire. He continued staring at it until he heard sirens coming from the driveway. After a final glance, he tucked it away in a deep, inside pocket of his winter jacket.

He walked away from the firepit and found the nearest Adirondack chair. He sat down, pulling out his notebook. With the frozen heart cold against his chest, the words for his next great work of folklore–now a true story–flowed effortlessly onto the page.

He was interrupted by the whining of dragonflies, calling out from the water. "Alannn…"

# ACKNOWLEDGMENTS

This story, a blend of extensive research and fast-paced folklore horror, was born from a desire to explore the chilling reality behind ancient legends.

I am deeply grateful to Crypsis Press for providing a home for this work. Their expertise was instrumental in transforming a rough concept into a polished reality; they remain a vital sanctuary for the weird, the new, and the unsettling.

To my family: this book wouldn't exist without you. Our time at a secluded cabin in New York—sharing campfires and chasing the northern lights—provided the spark for Insatiable. To my friends and family who served as first readers, thank you for the vital feedback that shaped this story.

I also want to thank the Crypsis Collective. This community provides an essential space for authors to explore their creativity with the support of a dedicated network of writers and readers.

Finally, to the readers: thank you for stepping into the woods with me.

# STAY CONNECTED

**Stay Connected with Evan Couchot**

Whether it's unearthing ancient folklore horror, deconstructing a complex mystery, or exploring the far reaches of science fiction, Evan's work explores the darker side of human behavior. Join Evan's personal newsletter for updates on the ongoing work, behind-the-scenes research, and news on upcoming releases across all genres. **Join the Author's Circle at www.CrypsisPress.com**

**The Crypsis Collective**

Crypsis Press LLC is more than a publisher—it is a mission to build better worlds through fiction. By joining the **Crypsis Collective**, you'll gain access to the official press newsletter, featuring first-look reveals at our expanding catalog, limited edition announcements, and exclusive community content. **Enter the Crypsis Collective** at www.CrypsisPress.com

# ABOUT THE AUTHOR

**Evan Couchot** lives at the intersection of what we know and what we fear. From the quiet streets of Mason, Ohio, to the laboratories of Boston, his work is defined by a fascination with the natural world and the mechanics of life.

As a biotechnology professional with degrees in Biology and Biotechnology, Evan brings a high degree of technical realism to his fiction. His stories—spanning deep-space science fiction, folklore mystery, and pharmaceutical-themed thrillers—are rooted in a deep understanding of the living world. Evan currently lives and works in Boston, where the city's history and innovation provide constant inspiration for his next mystery.

# ALSO BY EVAN COUCHOT

NOVELS:

*Makan*

*Adverse Events (coming 2026)*

www.ingramcontent.com/pod-product-compliance
Lightning Source LLC
LaVergne TN
LVHW040106080526
838202LV00045B/3801